This igloo book belongs to:

. . . .

igloobooks

Published in 2020
First published in the UK by Igloo Books Ltd
An imprint of Igloo Books Ltd
Cottage Farm, NN6 0BJ, UK
Owned by Bonnier Books
Sveavägen 56, Stockholm, Sweden
www.igloobooks.com

1020 002
2 4 6 8 10 9 7 5 3
ISBN 978-1-78905-685-3

Written by Melanie Joyce
Illustrated by César Samaniego

Designed by Justine Ablett
Edited by Stephanie Moss

Printed and manufactured in China

Santa CANCELS Christmas

igloobooks

It was nearly Christmas at the North Pole and Santa was feeling stressed.
It was time for a practice sleigh ride and he was trying to get dressed.

DECEMBER

But Santa had munched all the cookies and his suit was far too tight.

"Oh, dear," said Mrs Claus, smiling. **"He'll be in a bad mood tonight."**

Santa finally squeezed into his clothes and climbed into the sleigh.
"Now, behave, reindeer," he warned as they flew up, up and AWAY!

"He's so heavy!" moaned the reindeer.
Santa began to pout.
Then suddenly a lightning bolt
made his satnav go out!

"Oh, that's just great," said Santa. **"Now where do we go?"**
But without satellite directions, the reindeer didn't know.

Soon everyone was arguing and
Santa huffed and groaned.
The sleigh flew on for miles as the
reindeer squabbled and moaned.

"That's it, I resign," said Santa. **"I'm cancelling Christmas, too."**
The reindeer stopped in mid-air. They didn't know what to do.

Santa sat in a deck chair and put a handkerchief on his head.

"I'll have a strawberry ice cream and a fruity drink," he said.

While Santa splashed in the sea, some of the reindeer hatched a plan.
"We've got to tell Mrs Claus and get word to her if we can."

"**Help us save Christmas,**" said one, to a friendly-looking parrot.
"**We'll give you some jingly bells and half a juicy carrot.**"

The parrot flew to the North Pole.
He said, **"Brrr, it's so chilly here."**
Then he told Mrs Claus the story
of Santa and the reindeer.

Mrs Claus wrote Santa a note, saying, **"Enjoy your break, please do.**
But if you cancel Christmas, there'll be no presents for you."

BEARS

GAMES

VEHICLES

DOLLS

Meanwhile, on the beach, Santa soon got tired of the sun.
He thought about the children's presents and all the Christmas fun.

When Santa got the note, he said, **"Oh, dear. I'm really in trouble."**
So he jumped into the sleigh and flew off, on the double.

Back at the North Pole, Mrs Claus gave Santa a very hard time.
She put him on a diet and said cancelling Christmas was a crime.

Santa did lots of chores and hardly ate any pies.

Before too long he found himself back to his normal size.

So it was that Christmas
wasn't cancelled after all.
The children got their presents
when Santa Claus came to call.

Santa was forgiven and everyone had lots of fun.

"Ho-ho-ho!" said Mrs Claus. **"Merry Christmas, everyone!"**